REGINA is NOT a little DINOSAUR

by Andrea Zuill

schwartz & wade books · new york

Deep in the primeval forest
lurks a dangerous predator.
Her name is Regina.

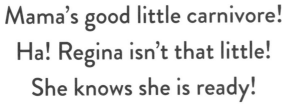

Mama's good little carnivore!
Ha! Regina isn't that little!
She knows she is ready!

Regina already has a terrifying roar,

a fear-inducing stare,

and an uncanny gift
for camouflage.

So after making sure her mom is well out of sight,
Regina heads off on her first real hunt, all by herself.

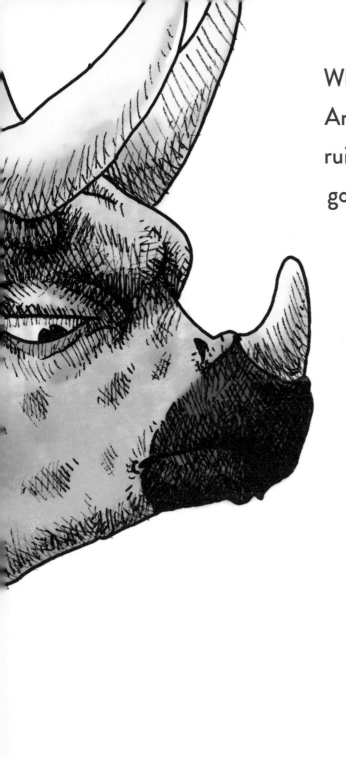

Whoa! That could have been dangerous! And a snack that size would have totally ruined her appetite for dinner. Regina is going to have to be much more careful.

So she waits . . .

and waits . . .

until she catches a scent!

Yes! This is more like it.

Hunting is turning out to be harder than Regina thought!

Regina is worried.

Why isn't she good at it?

What if she never gets good at it?

What if she has to live the

rest of her life as . . .

an HERBIVORE?!

Gasp!

What if . . . ?

SNAP!

Wait a minute. This might work! This creature is snack sized and doesn't have a hard shell.

This snack is hungry!

Mom is angry.

But she forgives Regina.

BOOP!

And since Regina is so eager,
Mom agrees to make her a list of things
that are safe to hunt.
Regina promises to follow it.

And she does.

This book is dedicated to
kids who are NOT too little
to achieve their goals.

Library of Congress Cataloging-in-Publication Data
Names: Zuill, Andrea, author, illustrator.
Title: Regina is not a little dinosaur / Andrea Zuill.
Description: New York: Schwartz & Wade Books, [2021] | Audience: Ages 3–7. | Audience: Grades K–1. |
Summary: Regina, a young dinosaur who is convinced she is ready to hunt for her own food, sneaks away from Mama,
but soon finds she has much to learn about hunting.
Identifiers: LCCN 2020012086 | ISBN 978-0-593-12728-5 (hardcover) | ISBN 978-0-593-12729-2 (library binding)
ISBN 978-0-593-12730-8 (ebook)
Subjects: CYAC: Dinosaurs—Fiction. | Hunting—Fiction.
Classification: LCC PZ7.1.Z83 Reg 2021 | DDC [E]—dc23
ISBN 978-0-593-12728-5 (trade) — ISBN 978-0-593-12729-2 (lib. bdg.) — ISBN 978-0-593-12730-8 (ebook)
Subjects: CYAC: Dinosaurs—Fiction. | Hunting—Fiction.
Classification: LCC PZ7.1.Z83 Reg 2021 | DDC [E]—dc23

The text of this book is set in Brandon Grotesque.
The illustrations were rendered in ink, scanned, and colored digitally.
MANUFACTURED IN CHINA
2 4 6 8 10 9 7 5 3 1
First Edition
Random House Children's Books supports the First Amendment and celebrates the right to read.